This
PJ BOOK
belongs to

_____

_____

PJ Library®

JEWISH BEDTIME STORIES and SONGS

Library of Congress Cataloging-in-Publication Data

Kimmelman, Leslie.
Sam & Charlie (and Sam too!) / Leslie Kimmelman ;
illustrated by Stefano Tambellini.
p. cm.
Summary: A boy named Sam, a girl named Charlie,
and Charlie's sister Sam become neighbors and friends.
ISBN 978-0-8075-7213-9
[1. Friendship—Fiction. 2. Jews—United States—Fiction.] I. Tambellini,
Stefano, ill. II. Title. III. Title: Sam and Charlie (and Sam too!).
PZ7.K56493Sam 2013
[E]—dc23
2012014113

The design is by Nick Tiemersma.

For more information about Albert Whitman & Company,
visit our web site at www.albertwhitman.com.

081324K1

SAM *and* CHARLIE

(AND SAM TOO!)

Leslie Kimmelman

Illustrated by
Stefano Tambellini

Albert Whitman & Company
Chicago, Illinois

TABLE OF CONTENTS

Love your neighbor as yourself.
–Leviticus 19:18

THE NEW NEIGHBORS

A new family moved in next door. Sam watched from his tree house. Well, maybe *watched* wasn't the right word. But he *listened* carefully. Finally Sam heard what he had been waiting for.

"Charlie, don't forget your baseball mitt!"

"Charlie, stay where I can see you!"

"Charlie, time to come in for lunch!"

Sam climbed down from the tree house, hurried next door, and rang the bell. A girl about his age opened the door.

"Hi, I'm your neighbor," said Sam. "Where's Charlie?"

"Here," said the girl.

"Here where?" said Sam.

"Me!" said the girl. "I'm Charlie."

"No way," said Sam. "Charlie is a boy's name." He looked down at Charlie's baseball mitt. "Isn't it?"

"I was named for my great-grandmother Charlene," explained Charlie. "But I'm warning you: *Never* call me Charlene."

"Who's this?" asked a smaller girl, coming up behind Charlie.

"I'm Sam," answered Sam.

"No way," said the girl. "That's a girl's name."

"Sam, meet my little sister," said Charlie. "She's Sam too, named after Great-Grandma Samantha."

Sam grinned. "Welcome to the neighborhood, Charlie and Sam Too," he said. "How about a game of catch?"

SHARING

"Is that hamentaschen?" said Charlie, coming into the backyard to play. "I love hamentaschen."

"My mom made them for Purim," answered Sam. "The first batch of holiday cookies. You want one?"

Charlie looked at the plate. "You got the last prune, and that's my favorite kind."

"Apricot's good too," said Sam.

"Prune's better," said Charlie. "Can I share?"

Sam looked at the hamentaschen. He looked at his friend. He looked at the hamentaschen again and slowly bit off one corner. "Your turn."

Charlie bit off the second corner. "Yum! Now what? There's only one corner left, but there are two of us."

"*My* mother baked them," said Sam. "So *I* should get the last bite."

"No," said Charlie. "If your mom bakes them, that means you get to taste them all the time. So *I* should get the last bite."

"I'm the oldest," said Sam. "So *I* should get the last bite."

"You're only two days older," said Charlie. "And I'm the one who's new in town. So *I* should get the last bite."

"Not so new anymore," said Sam. "Besides, I'm taller. So *I* should get the last bite."

Sam Too wandered over from next door. "Mmm. Hamentaschen. But only apricot is left? I like the prune kind best."

Sam looked at Charlie. Charlie looked at Sam.

Sam Too got the last bite of prune hamentaschen. "Thanks, guys. Happy Purim!"

SICK DAY

Charlie was sick in bed. "There's nothing to do," she muttered, "and no one to do it with." It was the middle of the day, and everyone else was outside playing.

There was a knock on her bedroom door. "Who is it?" called Charlie.

"It's me," said Sam, peering in. "I brought some chicken soup to make you feel better."

"Thank you, Sam," said Charlie. "But my stomach hurts. You eat it."

So Sam ate the soup. He felt much better.

"I almost forgot," said Sam. "These flowers are for you too."

Achoo! Achoo! Charlie sneezed right in Sam's face.

"Yuck!" said Sam. "You didn't turn away."

"I didn't have time," said Charlie. "Thanks for the flowers. But I'm allergic.

Why don't you put them in the kitchen?"

When Sam returned, he was holding a book.

"How about if I read to you?" he said. "This book is great. It always makes me feel better." He started to read. Charlie was fast asleep by page two.

So Sam read to himself. The book made him feel better.

When Charlie woke up, she felt better too.

"Thanks, Sam," she told her friend.

"Thanks for what?" Sam asked. "I didn't do anything."

"Yes, you did," said Charlie. "Friendship is the best medicine."

THE BAD HAIRCUT

Charlie got a new haircut the day before camp began. It didn't turn out exactly the way she had planned.

19

When Sam saw it, he couldn't believe his eyes. "What happened to your hair?" he asked. "It looks electric or something."

Charlie burst into tears and ran inside.

Sam didn't know what he'd done. "I told the truth," he said. "It *does* look electric."

At camp the next day, Charlie wore a baseball cap. She wouldn't talk to Sam.

Not at soccer. Not at T-ball. Not at arts and crafts. Music was Sam's favorite, but singing "Cheery Bim" was definitely not as much fun without Charlie.

The last activity of the day was free swim.
"See all those rings on the bottom of the
pool?" asked the counselor. "There's a prize
for the camper who gets the most rings!"

Sam was an underwater expert. He got seven rings right away. "I think that's probably the most," he told himself.

Charlie was good underwater too. She had six rings.

But now it looked like all the rings were taken.

As Sam was counting his rings again, one slipped out of his hand and floated down to the bottom of the pool.

"Hey, there's one more left!" called Charlie, pointing.

Sam *could* have said, "That's mine."

He *could* have won the prize.

But then he thought about what he'd said when he saw Charlie's electric hair.

Charlie dove to the bottom. She won the prize for the most rings collected.

But Sam felt like a winner too.

I'M SORRY DAY

Every year in the fall was a day the grown-ups called Yom Kippur. Sam called it I'm Sorry Day, because that's what you were supposed to say to everyone. When he

came back from synagogue that morning, he
saw Charlie was back from her synagogue
too, and she was sitting on the back porch.

"Hi Charlie," he said. "I'm sorry."

"Huh?" said Charlie. "What are you sorry
for?"

"I don't know," said Sam. "It's Yom Kippur—I'm Sorry Day. I'm just supposed to be sorry today."

"Hmm," said Charlie. "You're not very good at this. You're supposed to be sorry *for* something. Like, I'm sorry I sneezed in your face that time when I was sick. I really *did* have time to turn away. I just forgot."

"Oh, I get it," said Sam. "Okay. I'm sorry if I hurt your feelings when I laughed at your new haircut."

"*If* you hurt my feelings?" said Charlie. "That's not very sorry."

"*When* I hurt your feelings," said Sam.

"Better," said Charlie. "But it *was* an awful haircut." She giggled.

"It sure was," agreed Sam. "Hee hee hee."

"Ha ha ha." Charlie pulled her hair down over her eyes with one hand, and straight up in the back with the other. "Ha ha ha ha!"

"Hee hee hee hee," laughed Sam, making his hair stick up too. "Hee hee hee hee." He fell on the floor, holding his stomach and laughing himself silly.

"Ha ha ha ha ha," laughed Charlie, rolling on the floor. "Stop! Stop! Stop making me laugh!"

Sam Too came onto the back porch. "What's so funny?" she asked.

"Yom Kippur," answered Charlie, still cracking up. "It's hilarious!"

"Not really," said Sam Too.

Charlie and Sam stopped laughing. They stood up. They promised each other they'd try harder and be even better friends in the coming year.

"But make a *few* mistakes," said Charlie. "We need something to laugh about next I'm Sorry Day."

THE END